#1 Spider Stampede

Books in the
S.W.I.T.C.H. series

#1 Spider Stampede

Ali Sparkes

illustrated by
Ross Collins

MINNEAPOLIS

Text © Ali Sparkes 2011
Illustrations © Ross Collins 2011

"SWITCH: Spider Stampede" was originally published in English in 2011. This edition is published by an arrangement with Oxford University Press.

Copyright © 2013 by Darby Creek

Darby Creek
A division of Lerner Publishing Group, Inc.
241 First Avenue North
Minneapolis, MN 55401 U.S.A.

Website address: www.lernerbooks.com

Main body text set in ITC Goudy Sans Std. 14/19.
Typeface provided by Monotype Typography.

Library of Congress Cataloging-in-Publication Data

Sparkes, Ali.
    Spider stampede / by Ali Sparkes ; illustrated by Ross Collins.
      p. cm. — (S.W.I.T.C.H. ; #01)
    Summary: While seeking their lost dog, Piddle, twins Josh and Danny encounter their next-door neighbor, Petty Potts, a mad scientist whose SWITCH spray accidentally turns them into spiders.
    ISBN 978–0–7613–9199–9 (lib. bdg. : alk. paper)
    [1. Spiders—Fiction. 2. Brothers—Fiction. 3. Twins—Fiction.
4. Science fiction.] I. Collins, Ross, ill. II. Title.
PZ7.S73712Spi 2013
    [Fic]—dc23   2012026631

Manufactured in the United States of America
1 – SB – 12/31/12

For Naill

Danny and Josh
(and Piddle)

They may be twins, but they're NOT the same! Josh loves insects, spiders, beetles, and bugs. Danny can't stand them. Anything little with multiple legs freaks him out. So sharing a bedroom with Josh can be ... erm ... interesting. Mind you, they both love putting earwigs in big sister Jenny's underwear drawer ...

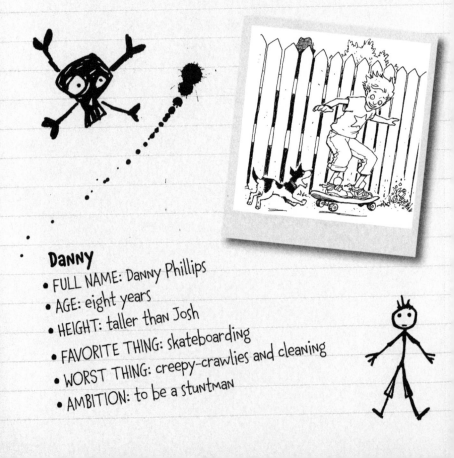

Danny
- FULL NAME: Danny Phillips
- AGE: eight years
- HEIGHT: taller than Josh
- FAVORITE THING: skateboarding
- WORST THING: creepy-crawlies and cleaning
- AMBITION: to be a stuntman

Josh
- FULL NAME: Josh Phillips
- AGE: eight years
- HEIGHT: taller than Danny
- FAVORITE THING: collecting insects
- WORST THING: skateboarding
- AMBITION: to be an entomologist

Piddle
- FULL NAME: Piddle the dog Phillips
- AGE: two dog years (fourteen in human years)
- HEIGHT: not very
- FAVORITE THING: chasing sticks
- WORST THING: cats
- AMBITION: to bite a squirrel

Contents

Losing Piddle

"AARRGGHH!!!!

GETITOFF! GETITOFF! GETITOFFMEEEE!!!!"

Josh looked up from his book. He saw his twin brother running around in circles by the hedge. He was wearing nothing but swimming trunks and a look of panic.

Actually, that's not true.

He was also wearing a spider.

"DON'T just sit there!" squeaked Danny. He whirled around. "Get it OFF!"

Josh sighed. He put his book down on the grass. It was amazing, he thought, that the spider could possibly hang on while his brother was thrashing about so wildly. It was a garden spider and quite large. Probably female. It had run up Danny's arm when he went to pick up his water pistol. Then it had scampered over his shoulder. Josh knew this because of the kind of dance his brother had just done across the grass. A sort of backward shimmy, with gasps of horror. Followed by wildly flapping arms and then the whirling as his unwelcome passenger legged it down his shoulder blade.

"You could win the Under Nines Dancing Championship," Josh said. He dodged under a flailing arm to scoop up the dizzy spider. It was now hanging onto the waistband of Danny's trunks.

"Very funny!" squealed Danny. "Have you got it? Is it gone?!"

"Yes, calm down. Look! She's a beauty!" Josh cupped the spider in his hands. He held it out for Danny to see. It was nut brown with mottled yellow patterns on its back.

"NOOO! Get it away from me!"

"But look! She's got these amazing feet that can hook on to stuff while she's hanging upside down and—"

"Just STOP talking about the S-P-I-D-E-R!" growled Danny. He shuddered and refused to

look. Josh gently dropped it behind the shed.

"She'll be back over by the hedge again in no time," said Josh. This didn't comfort his twin much. "Along with all the others. You're never more than a few feet away from a spider, you know."

"Not *one* more *word* about . . . those . . . *things*!"

Josh pushed his hands into his shorts pockets

and grinned. "Mandibles," he muttered, quietly. He didn't think Danny would know what this word was. He'd read only yesterday that mandibles were what spiders used for eating. Not teeth exactly. Just sort of munchy parts on their faces.

Danny hated anything creepy-crawly. For twins, he and Josh were very different. Josh was fascinated by small creatures and bugs. He had tons of wildlife books. He used to bring woodlice, snails, and beetles into the house. But Jenny, their older sister, found earwigs in her hair dryer. Then Danny screamed loud enough to wake the dead after stepping into his brother's box of centipedes when he got up to go to the bathroom in the middle of the night. So Mom said Josh could only look at bugs and stuff outside. It was probably just as well. If Jenny didn't squash them flat with a sandal, Mom would suck them up in the vacuum cleaner. Or Piddle would eat them. Piddle, their scruffy little terrier (named after a habit he had when he got overexcited), liked nothing more than to munch up a spider if he spotted one sauntering by.

"How can you *like* those things?" Danny asked. He pulled his shorts and T-shirt on over his swimming trunks. He'd soured on the wading pool. Too many dead flies in it. "Ewww! I wish there weren't any insects in the world!"

"One, spiders aren't insects—they're arachnids," said Josh. He climbed up the jungle gym. "And two, if there were no insects in the world, we would all die out. The human race depends on them."

"You freaky little bug geek!" muttered Danny.

"Lucky for you that I *do* like them!" added Josh. "Or we'd *both* be screaming and wiggling all over the garden right now."

Danny ignored him. He checked his spiky fair hair with a shiver just in case another spider had dropped in. Josh's hair was short and neat. He wouldn't mind a spider in it at all. How could twins be so different? wondered Danny. He pulled on his sneakers. He loved playing computer games and listening to loud music. Josh would rather play with newts and listen to birdsong.

But Danny had to admit he was useful for creepy-crawly removal.

Danny abandoned the water pistol and picked
up his skateboard. Soon he was racing up and
down the path. Piddle was racing along beside
him, yapping and nearly tripping him up every ten
seconds.

Upstairs from Jenny's bedroom window a pop
tune thumped loudly. From the kitchen poured the
burble of daytime TV, which their mom liked to
watch while she did the ironing.

From the other side of the high wooden fence,
there came a thump. And then another thump.
And then a crotchety voice. "*Will* you all shut up!
I'd have a quieter afternoon on the main runway
at the airport!" Josh grimaced. It was Miss Potts,

who lived in the run-down red brick house next door. People thought she was a bit eccentric. An old witch more like, thought Josh.

"I SAID," came the voice again, louder. "Will you all SHUT UP?!"

But Mom and Jenny and Danny and Piddle were all making way too much noise to hear. "Sorry, Miss Potts," said Josh. He felt embarrassed. "I'll ask them to be quieter."

"Oh, don't bother!" she snapped back. The top of her tweedy hat was the only thing he could see over the fence. "I'll soon be deaf and then it won't matter!"

Josh waved at Danny and mouthed, "Miss Potts!"

Danny skidded his skateboard to a halt, shaking his head. Piddle sat back on his furry bottom. He waited, wiggling impatiently, for the fun to start again.

Josh ran past him and pushed the kitchen window shut. At once the noise from Mom's TV program dropped. He could still hear Miss Potts though, just on the other side of the fence. She was muttering, "Remember! Remember! *Oh, you stupid old biddy!* Remember! Where did you hide them? Where?"

Josh bent down. He peered through a knothole in the wood. He saw the old lady crawling along through the weeds, which were nearly as tall as he was, obviously searching for something. Then she suddenly bobbed up. She thwacked her hand hard against her forehead and snapped, "STUPID old woman! Had to go and get your brain burnt out, didn't you?" Then she stood up and stomped off into her ramshackle garden shed.

It was right what they said about Petty Potts, Josh decided. She really was crazy.

"She's always moaning about noise!" Danny said, suddenly, right in his ear. Josh jumped. "Does she think this is a library or something? It's a freakin' yard! Kids play in yards. Dogs play in yards!" And he picked up a rubber ball and threw it for Piddle. "There you go, Piddle! Catch!"

Piddle hurtled down the path. He threw himself into the pile of yard clippings and compost in the far corner. "Don't pay any attention to her. Old whiny pants," said Danny. "Come on, Piddle! Here, boy!"

They glanced back across the yard expecting to see Piddle foraging through the leaves and cut grass. Then they both blinked and stared back at each other in surprise.

Piddle had vanished.

Turning Yellow

"Look, there's a hole! He must have squeezed through," grunted Josh. He was almost upside down in the compost pile. "He's gone next door!"

"Can we get through after him?" asked Danny. He peered over Josh's shoulder and eyed the compost pile warily. It was *full* of horrible things, he knew. Worms, beetles, ants, spiders . . . ugh.

"Maybe—if we wriggle . . ." said Josh.

"Or should we just go over and knock and ask for him back?" Danny said, hopefully. He *really* didn't want to get personal with that heap of horrors.

"What—like a lost ball?" scoffed Josh. "We've never got one of *those* back from her before, have we? No . . . I think . . . we can almost . . ."

Josh wriggled and dug down through the warm,

moist dirt and leaves between the back of the compost pile and the fence. The wood around the small hole was old and rotten. As Josh pushed against it, more fell away. He squeezed his head and shoulders through, getting a face full of overgrown grass. Then he crawled right into Miss Potts's yard. With a few grunts and complaints, Danny followed. He tried not to notice anything scuttling in the heap. The tickly feeling on his skin was just grass . . . probably. With a squeak of revulsion, he knocked off a centipede. Then he hurtled through the gap after Josh, grazing his left ear.

"Piddle! Piddle!" Josh was calling, softly. No

reply. No patter of little clawed feet. No yap.

The weeds grew up to their waists, filled with invisible chirruping grasshoppers. As Josh and Danny crawled through the high grass and nettles, they heard one shrill little bark. "He's in her shed!" gasped Danny.

"And *she's* in there!" said Josh, with a gulp. "She'll be going nuts! We have to go in and rescue him."

The shed door was open. They tiptoed in. At first it all looked quite normal. There was a rake propped up by the door. A wheelbarrow under some old shelves, full of gardening stuff. An old sheet was hung up on nails at the back.

"It doesn't *smell* like a shed," whispered Danny. "It smells like . . . like . . . "

"Like school," said Josh. "Sort of . . . " But he couldn't figure out exactly why.

"Yes . . . something at school," agreed Danny, not bothering to whisper now. "But they're not in here, are they?"

Then there was another bark. It was *definitely* coming from *inside* the shed. Danny and Josh

stared at each other in confusion. Then Danny
strode to the back wall, grabbed the old sheet
hanging on the nails, and pulled it aside. Behind it
was a red metal door.

The door was ajar. Pushing it open, Danny
saw gray stone steps leading a short way down
to a passage. "Come on!" Danny went through.
Josh followed, staring around him. Wobbly
metal panels—corrugated iron, thought Josh—
curved up over them in an arch. At the end of

the passage was a well-lit room as big as their bedroom and Jenny's put together. And in the middle of it, right ahead of them, was a sort of square plastic see-through tent. And in the middle of *that* was Piddle.

The room smelled strange. Very strange. It still reminded him of school. Like the room where they did science. And there was a hissing noise. Piddle was standing very still with the fur on his back sticking up. He was scared. "It's all right, Piddle. We've found you!" said Danny. And pushing the plastic sheeting open, he went into the strange tent. Josh gave a swift glance around, noticing some odd machinery and a kind of glass booth, glowing green, off to the left. He hurried in after Danny.

"Come on. Let's get out of here! It gives me the heebie-jeebies," he said. Danny gathered the shivering Piddle up into his arms.

Then the hissing got louder. Something cool sprayed across their bare legs.

"What was *that* . . . ?" gasped Danny.

"Don't know! Don't care! Let's go!" replied Josh.

They pushed out of the weird tent thing.

Suddenly, Miss Potts's voice rang out. "Who's that! Who's in my lab?"

Danny grabbed Josh's arm. They hurtled back along the dark, damp passage.

"HEY! STOP! Come back here!" yelled Miss Potts. They could hear her thumping across the wooden floor of the weird secret room behind them.

Josh and Danny leapt up the steps, two at a time. Piddle yelped excitedly over Danny's shoulder. His ears were flapping around, and his pink tongue was hanging out.

"STOP! I know who you ARE!" bellowed Miss Potts.

Danny, Josh, and Piddle almost fell into the garden. Miss Potts's bony hand swatted the sack curtain aside behind them.

"RUN!" gasped Danny. "RUN!"

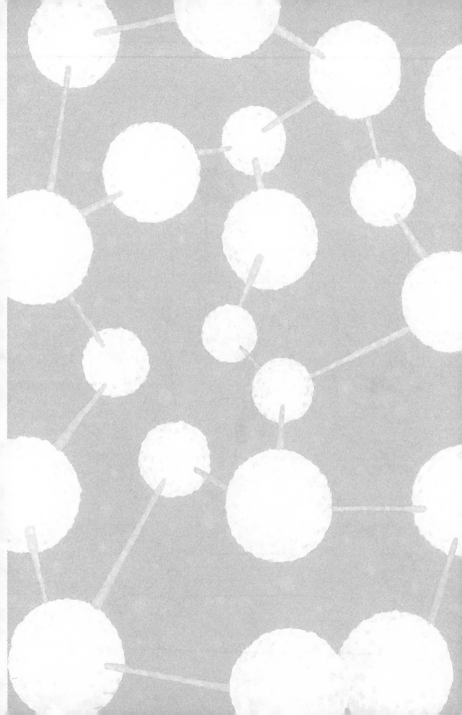

Too Many Knees

They hurtled back through the overgrown weeds. They shoved Piddle under the fence and scrambled after him as fast as they could go.

Back on their own side, they didn't stop running. Josh and Danny belted straight into the house and upstairs, as if a wild beast was chasing them. It wasn't until they got to the landing that they collapsed in a heap and started to laugh. Piddle sniffed at their legs and sneezed. Then he trotted off into their bedroom.

"Ugh!" Danny peered at his legs. They looked kind of . . . yellow. And they had that weird smell they'd noticed in the secret laboratory. Josh's legs were also covered in the same strange liquid.

"Come on—let's get this stuff off!" said Josh. They clattered into the bathroom.

"Hey! Don't you two go in there! I'm just about to take my bath!" yelled Jenny, from her bedroom.

"We won't be long!" called back Josh. "Two minutes!"

They took off their shoes and socks and rolled up their shorts. They stood up in the big bathtub.

"What *is* this stuff?" Danny wrinkled his nose.

"Whatever it is, it's coming off," said Josh. He grabbed the shower attachment but dropped it.

Then the bath started to grow . . .

Its curved metal rim suddenly shot high, high up beyond their heads. The flat base with its little square of antislip bumps suddenly stretched out beneath and around them until it was the size of a basketball court and the bumps were small hills.

"AAAAAAaaaaa!" . . .

. . . commented Josh.
And Danny agreed.

The plug was now the size of a playground merry-go-round. It was hanging off a chain that wouldn't have looked out of place attached to the anchor of a warship.

"AAAAAH!" added Josh.

Danny went along with that.

At last the growing seemed to stop. They were in a vast white valley of bathtub.

"What's going on?" whimpered Danny. "What happened to the bathtub?" His voice sounded a bit funny. Sort of raspy. And his eyes felt very odd. He seemed to be able to see around corners at the same time as straight ahead . . .

Behind him came Josh's voice—also a bit raspy. "Um . . . Danny. Promise me you'll stay calm." Josh stared into the shiny mirrorlike top of the giant shower attachment. It was leaning against the side of the incredibly huge bath. He gulped and blinked some eyes. Yep. His reflection was still the same. He wasn't dreaming it.

"What *is* that?" Danny found himself moving, rather smoothly and swiftly, he thought, toward a huge round well. Above it rested the immense

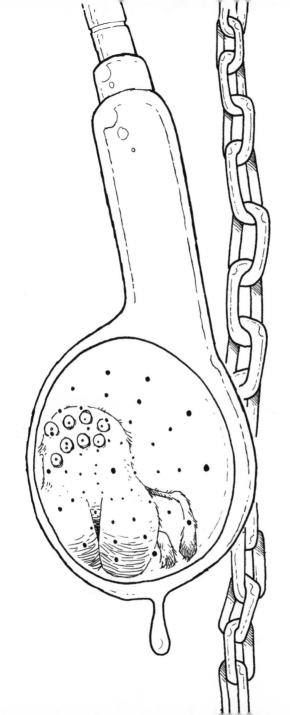

plug on its gigantic chain. The top of the plug
was also shiny and mirrorlike. In it Danny saw
something huge and hairy and standing high on
eight legs. It had eight eyes and a rather surprised
expression. And it MUST BE RIGHT ON TOP OF
HIM!!!!!

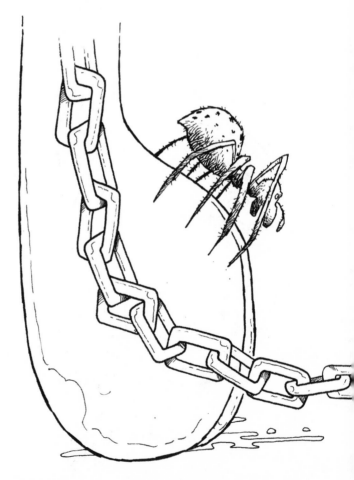

"JO-O-SH! GETITOFF! GETITOFF! GETITOFFMEEEE!!!!" screamed Danny, freaking out. The spider was freaking out too. It waved its hairy legs wildly in the giant plug mirror just beyond the giant plughole.

"I can't get it off you, you dingbat," shouted Josh. "It *is* you!"

Danny's mandibles quivered. He looked around. He saw yet another spider over by the showerhead where Josh's voice was coming from. His eight eyes rolled up. At least sixteen knees went weak. Then, in a tangle of legs, he fainted.

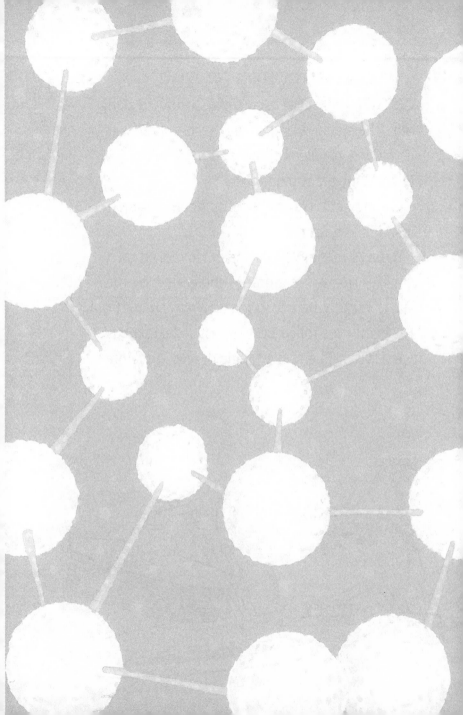

A Hairy Experience

Josh ran across to the collapsed body of his brother. He got hold of Danny's shoulder area—or "thorax" if he was being correct—using his palps (the little arms on either side of his head) and his two front legs.

"Danny! Wake up!" he shouted in his odd raspy voice. It was probably pointless, though. Danny would most likely just scream and faint again as soon as he saw his brother. Or his own reflection. Like it or not, believe it or not, they had both just turned into spiders. Josh's brain was doing backflips. He was trying to take this amazing fact in and work out how it had happened. But he didn't have much time for pondering. He heard a terrible low roaring sound that made the metal under his eight feet vibrate. A shadow fell across him, and he looked up to see a horrifying sight.

Jenny.

Screaming.

Raising her gargantuan right hand, in which was grasped a titanic sandal.

Jenny's scream came out incredibly slowly in a weird rumbly voice, as if she had a very sore throat.

"AAAAAH! SPIIIIIDEEEERRRRRSSS!"

Her blonde ponytail swung sideways in a huge slow swoop. Her eyes were large and round and shiny. Her vast gaping mouth looked like a terrifying gooey red tunnel.

Even though everything she did was in slow motion, the sandal was now halfway into Bathtub Valley and heading straight for them. They were about to be pulped.

"*Danneee!*" screamed Josh. He pulled his brother toward the drain. At last Danny's eyes opened. They started to roll up again as soon as they clapped themselves onto Josh. Josh cuffed Danny's mandibles with a spare palp and said, "Cut it out! Don't you dare faint again! We've got to run!"

Now the sandal was casting a deadly shadow over them. Josh could smell its rubber sole. He and Danny ran for it. They zipped across to the huge round black well. Then they teetered out on its metal crossbars for just a second before the sandal smashed down right next to them. A gust of rubbery wind knocked them both over. One second later, they were falling down the drain.

"AAAAARGH!" bellowed both spiders.

They were plummeting, legs flailing wildly
around them, into a dark, dark hole. Who knew
where it ended? wondered Josh, frantically. It
smelled like soap and old water. Spinning and
tumbling, Josh wondered what it would be like to
suffer eight broken legs. Or maybe have one come
off altogether. Spiders were always losing legs.
That had to hurt!

But the next moment he landed with a thud on something quite soft and springy. The moment after that, his brother landed on top of him.

"Where are we?" Danny whimpered.

"Down the drain," said Josh. He shoved one of Danny's legs off his face. "Obviously."

"But . . . where down the drain?"

Josh looked around. His eyesight was pretty good considering how dark it must be. But of course, most spiders were nocturnal. Out and about hunting by night. Danny had scrambled up onto his feet now. He was also staring down.

"Oh—oh yuck!" he said. "You know what this is? What we've landed in?"

"What?" Josh looked at the soggy matter underneath them. It looked like a rather sticky, oozy pile of tangled cables.

"It's Jenny's *hair*! That's what it is!"

Both boys shuddered. "All those times Mom told her not to let big clumps of hair go down the drain after her shower," said Danny. "She always said it plugged up the pipes. And now we know she was right. Yeeee-uk!"

"Good thing Jenny didn't pay any attention to Mom," said Josh. "Her hair gave us a soft landing. She saved our lives."

Danny shuddered as he looked at Josh. "Am I really a spider? Just like you? Or am I dreaming this?"

"Yep. You're just like me," said Josh. "And I think this is real."

"Oooow . . ." wailed Danny. "I was really hoping this was a dream! How can this be real? How can it?"

"Shhh!" said Josh, looking up into the dark. There was a gurgle above them.

"Ulp," said Danny.

"She might have saved our lives . . ." said Josh. There was a splosh.

"But she's trying to kill us again now!" he screamed. "She's turned on the FAUCET!"

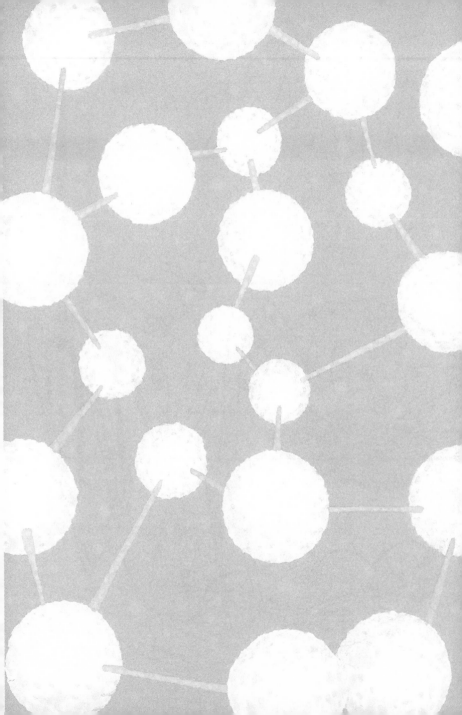

A Bit Drained

The water hit them in a big lump. It knocked them off the shelf of hair and on down through the dark pipe. Plunging down in a whirling, spinning cascade, Josh felt his legs flapping about in all directions. He prayed that a leg wouldn't snap off. Then there was a brief, brilliant flash of light. They shot out of the end of the downpipe that ran along the outside of the house. Then all was dark again as they were carried on down into the pipes that led to the sewer.

Splat! Danny hit a brick and lay draped soggily over the edge. Splodge! Josh landed on top of him. They were on a ledge of some kind. Above them the dark round hole of the pipe dumped still more water on them, but it was now a light shower. Then it dwindled to just a few drips.

Jenny must have put the plug in to fill up the bathtub, thought Josh.

Groaning, they gradually untangled their limbs. They got up into a sitting position. Below them was a sort of canal through which water slowly flowed. It smelled a bit rotten eggy to Josh. And not in a good way. It was dark, but a chink of light fed down from the world above them. He knew that spider sight meant they could see much better than they would have as boys.

"I don't like this," whimpered Danny.

"You don't say!" muttered Josh.

"Look," snapped Danny, "it's bad enough that you're a spider without being sarcastic too!"

"WE are spiders. Not just me!" grouched back Josh. He stepped over a toenail clipping the size of half a bike wheel.

"But—but how? How can this be happening?" gulped Danny. His eight eyes were wide and scared.

"It must have been that yellow stuff," said Josh.

"It's done something to us."

"And now we're stuck in a sewer with six more

legs than we ever wanted," groaned Danny. "And
I'm scared to death—of *me*!"

"There are other things you should be scared
of, mate!" came an unfamiliar voice. Danny and
Josh spun around to look. Then all the screaming
started again. Towering over them, with glittering
black eyes and sharp yellow teeth, was a huge
brown hairy monster.

Scratch and Sniff

"Oh, do give it a rest," said the monster. "We could hear you screaming all the way down the drainpipe. You should hear yourselves, honestly."

Josh and Danny stopped screaming. They just gulped and gasped a bit instead.

"My name's Scratch," said the monster. He held out a clawed paw. Danny stared at it. Josh carefully put out a leg to shake.

"And this 'ere is my missus—Sniff." Another, smaller, monster put her head around the furry shoulder of the first. She smiled kindly. "We live under your shed."

"Hello, love," Sniff said. "Don't look so scared. We won't bite."

"But . . . but . . . don't you want to eat us?" squeaked Danny.

Sniff made a face. "What—spider legs? Stuck in my teeth? I don't think so!"

"We're rats," went on Scratch. "We have more refined tastes. Don't you know? Now, a nice bit of *cake*—oooh yes!"

"Chocolate cake," sighed Sniff, dreamily. "With no frosting."

Rats! Of course. Now that they were slightly less terrified, Josh and Danny could make out the rodenty shape of Scratch and Sniff.

"And anyway—you're not *regular* spiders, are you?" said Scratch. He narrowed his beadlike black eyes.

"Can you tell?" gasped Josh.

"Oh yes. It's the smell," said Scratch. "And all the talking. Spiders aren't normally so chatty."

"You've been got, haven't you, love?" said Sniff. "By that mad scientist—Petty Potts."

Danny and Josh scuttled around. They exchanged sixteen blinks of surprise.

"Oh you needn't be surprised. We rats know a lot about what humans get up to!" said Scratch with an airy stroke of his whiskers. "We're your closest cousins, don't you know? Nobody else in the animal world more like humans than rats. We're omnivores and scavengers—just like you!"

"O . . . K," said Josh. "But what can you tell us about Petty Potts? Exactly *what* has she done to us?"

"It's her S.W.I.T.C.H. spray," said Scratch. "She's been working on it for years in that secret lab of hers. We pop in from time to time for the sandwiches (she never finishes a cheese-and-pickle sandwich!). Anyway, she finally made a breakthrough a few weeks ago. And she started to S.W.I.T.C.H. things!"

"*Switch* things?" said Danny.

"S-W-I-T-C-H," said Scratch. "It stands for . . . now . . . let me think . . ."

"Serum Which Instigates Total Cellular Hijack!" said Sniff. She suddenly sounded like a chemistry professor.

"Um . . . what?" said Danny.

"It's a serum. That's what she calls it," went on Sniff. "It forces all your body cells to be different kinds of cells. Like each cell has been hijacked by another cell, you see? So—Serum Which Instigates Total Cellular Hijack! We've only heard her say it about a 150 times! She spent ages trying to come up with a smart-sounding name. She was going to call it Serum To Initiate Process Of Morphing. But STIPOM just doesn't roll off the tongue so well."

"How do you *know* all these words?" gasped
Danny. "I mean . . . you're *rats*!"

"Danny!" Josh poked his brother with one hairy
leg. "Rats are very intelligent!"

"Well, we watch a lot of TV," said Sniff.

"Hear a lot of public radio too," said Scratch.

"Anyway, at first she was just doing little
things with this S.W.I.T.C.H. spray," went on

ended up—down the drain!" Scratch chuckled and shook his head. "And as your closest cousins, well, it was only right to try and help."

"Well ... er ... thanks," said Josh. He resisted the urge to correct Scratch. Apes were *actually* their closest cousins. But it seemed impolite to say so. "But what do we do now?"

"Well, get out of here for a start," said Scratch. "It's not safe. Get on our backs, and we'll swim you out of here." Doubtfully, the brothers looked at the rats' backs. Scratch and Sniff shimmied down low to let the spiders climb on board.

"Go on, love," Sniff encouraged Josh. "Just hang on to my fur, and you won't fall off."

Josh went for it. He just ran up Sniff's back. He found it surprisingly easy. There were clever little hooks on the bottom of each of his feet. They anchored him tightly onto her fur. Danny ran up onto Scratch a moment later. Then, with a whoosh of rotten eggy air, Scratch leapt into the slow-moving stream and began to swim along the sewer.

The dark water surged up. Danny ran up onto
Scratch's head, alarmed. It was quite flat on top
between his ears and easy to hang on to. Behind
swam Sniff, her nose held daintily above the
water. Josh was also anchored between her ears.

"Oh no—we're not going down to the bit where the poos come out, are we?" fretted Danny. But a moment later they came out into daylight. They were swimming through the small stream in the little overgrown gully, which ran along between the backyards on their road and the next road. "Phew! No poo!" sighed Danny.

"I should think *not*," sniffed Sniff. "We do have our standards, you know!"

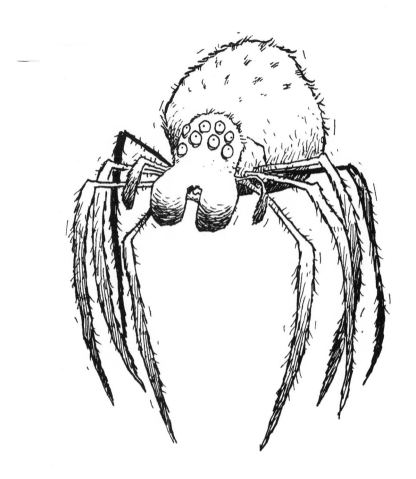

"Thank you," said Josh. He ran down Sniff's soaked back and onto a large stone at the edge of the stream. "Now can you tell us how we get back to being humans?"

Scratch and Sniff shook the water out of their fur on a tiny beach of pebbles below them. They exchanged worried glances as Danny joined Josh on the rock.

"You don't—you don't mean to tell us . . . that we're like this for good?" gasped Josh.

"Well . . . er . . . no," said Scratch. "We don't know that for sure. And in fact, I know that one of the bees turned back into a bee after just a few hours as an ant . . ."

"*One* of them? What happened to the other ones that Petty Potts got with her S.W.I.T.C.H. spray?" demanded Josh.

"Well—they *might* have changed back . . . if there had been time," said Scratch, looking rather awkward. "Only . . . well . . . most of them got . . ."

"Got? Got what?" squawked Danny. He stood up high on his legs like a very unattractive ballerina.

"Eaten," sighed Sniff. "Most things get eaten. I mean . . . a lot of things get eaten *anyway*. But when you're an ant or a bee or a beetle or something, you get to know how to look out for yourself. If you're suddenly S.W.I.T.C.H.ed into something else you get . . . well . . .

63

confused. And if you're confused, you're . . . well . . . lunch!"

"Josh," said Danny. He edged toward his brother even though he was still terrified of his legs.

"I don't know about you—but I'm confused. I'm *very* confused."

"Me too," gulped Josh. And that's when the icky, sticky pink thing suddenly ickily stickily stuck to his shoulder. And he was yanked high into the air.

Lunch

The worst thing about being a freaky little bug geek was knowing *too* much.

And the worst thing about being a spider was being able to think so much faster than a human. Josh had read, in his many wildlife books, that everything moves so much faster in the world of spiders and insects that they must think quickly to survive. And now he knew it was true, as he flew through the air, stuck to the pink thing. He had time to figure out quite a few things.

He figured out, first of all, that he was stuck to the tongue of a toad.

Then he figured out that he was probably not going to unstick himself.

Then he figured out that he was probably going to be eaten . . . ALIVE!

He knew that toads eat their prey alive. They don't mind at *all* if their lunch kicks and complains as it goes down. For the first time ever in his life, Josh wished he hadn't read so many wildlife books.

As he flew helplessly toward the toad's gaping mouth, Josh twisted around. He got ahold of some of the long, long tongue, drove his fangs into it, and squirted some venom in. The tongue didn't let go. There was no hope. He was toad takeout.

CRUNCH.
SPLAT.
SQUISH.

That's the end of me, thought Josh. *Funny. Only felt a little bump!* He opened one eye. Then six or seven more. The sticky tongue was still attached to his shoulder (or thorax, if he was being correct). But the other end was no longer attached to a toad. It lay flattened under a giant black boot.

Someone had stamped on the toad! STAMPED on it!

Behind him Josh could hear anguished cries from Danny and Scratch and Sniff. They must think he was done for. Josh stood up. He found all his legs were shaking with fright. Then he ran away before whoever it was could stamp on him too. The tongue followed him. Eeewwww! It came away from the edge of the boot. It snaked along behind him like a weird scarf. It skipped and bounced over the rocks and fallen trees, which had once been just twigs and pebbles when he was a boy.

As he reached Danny and their rat friends, Josh yelled—for the first time ever—"GETTITOFF! GETTITOFF! GETTITOFFMEEEEE!"

Scratch leaned over. He tugged the half a tongue with his teeth. It squelched and popped as it finally came off.

"We thought you was a goner, son!" said Scratch. He spit out the tongue and hustled them all beneath an old log. "We thought you was lunch! Nobody's ever got away from Gripper. Not ever! If he hadn't just got stamped on, you'd be down his throat by now."

Poor Josh gulped. Danny went to put a comforting arm . . . er . . . leg . . . around him . . . but just couldn't make that work somehow. (*Whoever got comfort from a spider's leg?* he wondered.) "We've *got* to find a way to get back to being humans again," he said. "Or we'll never make it to dinnertime."

"Well, I hate to say it," said Sniff. "But Petty Potts is most likely the only one who can help you."

"But how will she know it's us? She might just stamp on us like someone just stamped on that toad," squeaked Danny. He looked around, anxiously. The owner of the boot, who had been screened from view by the leaves of a large bush, seemed to have gone.

"No, she wouldn't stamp on you. She never wastes insects," said Scratch.

"Arachnids," corrected Josh. Everyone gave him a *look*.

"And didn't you see? It was Petty Potts who just stamped on Gripper," added Scratch. "She was probably after him for another one of her experiments." Scratch peered out from under the log. "She's made a gap in her back fence so she can get down here and kidnap innocent creatures for her lab! Can't see her now though. She must have gone back in with Gripper's gooey bits. I think we should take you back there too. Maybe she'll help you. Maybe you can find a way to show her who you are."

"Well, at least let's check for any more toads, before we go," said Josh, with a shiver.

He edged out from under the log and looked all around. Then he ran up a tree. Yes! He ran right up it so fast he shocked himself. "Look at me! Danny! Look at me! I'm up the tree!" he yelled, excitedly. He forgot to be afraid.

Danny lost no time in catching up. He was the athletic one, after all. He wasn't going to be beaten to the top by Josh. "Woo-hoo!" he called, overtaking Josh. "I'm a superhero! I can walk up walls!!!"

"Steady now," called up Scratch from the lower part of the trunk. He was scrabbling a little way

up. "Lots of things up there looking for lunch! Best come down."

But Josh and Danny had now run along to the tip of a high branch. They were staring, amazed, at the view. From here they could see across their yard and into the yards on either side. Everything lay below them like half the country, seen from an airplane. So incredibly colorful and interesting and BIG! Butterflies flapped past them like giant kites. Bees and flies zoomed in all directions, sounding like helicopters and never bumping into one another, as if they were being guided by air traffic control.

A slurping noise above them turned out to be a chubby green caterpillar munching through a leaf. It burped. It winked a big black eye at them. It went, "Pardon."

"Oooh—lovely! Leggy snackage! I was feeling peckish," came a voice just behind them. Danny spun about in horror. Above them on the branch was a humongous bird. A blackbird, he thought. It had a bright orange beak. And the beak was jabbing right down toward them.

"AAAAARGH!"

Danny ran up the branch and then found himself sliding off the edge. For one horrible second he tipped sideways into thin air, ready to plummet down. And then he realized he was still running. He ran right around under the branch, Josh hot on his many heels. All of a sudden, the world was upside down. Their incredible little hooky feet were keeping them attached to the craggy bark of the tree. They were defying gravity!

"Like Spider-Man!" marveled Josh, under his breath.

"Has it gone?" whispered Danny.

For a few seconds they hung there, petrified. Then there was a terrifyingly loud whistle. A huge black-feathered head swung around the branch and gaped its beak at them.

"Aah—nearly lost you," it said. "Brace yourself. Got the munchies."

"Noooooooo!" shouted both Josh and Danny. Below they could hear Scratch and Sniff desperately shouting at the bird to get away.

"Now look!" said the bird, tilting its head on one side and regarding them patiently. "Stop messing around. I need a snack and you're it. That's the pecking order. Get over it."

"Drop!" yelled Josh. "Just let go!"

Danny didn't need telling. He'd rather splatter on the ground than get eaten alive. He let go and found himself once again wheeling around in free fall.

Ooh. *That* was an unexpectedly soft landing.

As Danny lay dazed, he realized he was on some kind of material. A short distance away Josh was also flopped onto the material, feverishly counting his legs. Danny looked at the crisscross of green and brown wool threads. From its round shape and a few gray cables of hair on it, he guessed it was a hat. And now it was tipping up.

Shrieking, Josh and Danny ran up the material, grabbing hold after hold with their hooky feet. But whoever was holding the hat determinedly shook it until they fell again, this time with a plop, into a large see-through container. Inside it Josh ran around and around, shooting something weird out of his bottom.

"Eeeuw!" said Danny. "Spider-Man never did it like *that*!"

Josh was making an emergency web. He was shooting silk out of the spinner on his abdomen to create a network of strong rope, which he was sticking all over the see-through plastic at very high speed as he ran around. They would be able to use it to climb up.

But Danny could see it was hopeless. Above them a lid crashed down shut. And now the super-sized face of none other than Petty Potts loomed slowly into view, peering in at them. Josh could see mammoth bristly hairs up inside her cavernous pink nostrils.

He slumped down into his useless emergency web and sighed. "I really didn't ever want to see that."

A Bit of Gas

"OOOOOH DDDEEEEEEAR!" roared Petty Potts, in a slow deep voice.

"TIIIIIIME TOO GEEET YOUUUU FFFIIIIIXXEEED UUUUPPPP."

Josh felt quite seasick as their plastic tub swung along in the old lady's hands.

He clung on tightly to the stout see-through silk cables that he had unexpectedly produced. He was rather proud of his web, in fact. Even if it had come out of his backside.

Danny was hanging on too, his furry face looking rather green. "Now what?" he whimpered.

Josh thought hard. He didn't think Petty Potts would hurt them deliberately. But maybe she would want to experiment on them. After all, it

sounded as if she knew who they were. She must be pretty excited. She had succeeded in turning two mammals into spiders!

At last they reached the huge dark cave of her laboratory behind the shed. She set their tub down on a gigantic table and peeled off the lid. She spoke at them, but it was too roary and loud and slow to make any sense. Her big warm gusts of breath smelled like cheese.

A short while later, there were two thuds, and two dark bundles, wrapped in white material, bounced down between them. They smelled fantastic. Danny suddenly realized how incredibly hungry he was. These were flasks of hot meaty soup! He was sure of it. He could smell it. He scuttled across to one of them and quickly ripped off the wrapping. The flask had six legs, two wings, and an anxious expression. But Danny didn't stop to think about this. Yum! The soup was great!

It was only when he'd gulped it all down that he noticed the look on Josh's face. His brother's mandibles were stuck up straight like shocked fingers. One of his eyes twitched. "Nice lunch?" he whispered.

"Ah . . . yes," admitted Danny. "Er . . . bluebottle soup. Not Mom's, but not bad." He shuddered and felt a little queasy.

"ARGH!" said Josh and Danny agreed with him. The tub was tipping up, and they were sliding out onto the tabletop. The surface was cold stone of some kind. Quite smooth. Now a glass bowl was slammed, upside down, over them. Through a round gap in the top, a yellowish fog was hissing and blooming down.

"She's killing us! We're done for!" whimpered Danny. But Josh thought he was wrong. It would be much easier to kill them with a shoe than with gas. A few seconds later, though, he wasn't so sure. His head felt funny and his legs gave way and his ears were all muffled and . . . and . . . and . . .

"Can't say I ever thought you two would be welcome in my lab. But today has changed my

mind and no mistake," said Petty Potts. She had stopped roaring and her mammoth face was now back to its usual size, Danny realized. He sat up, his legs—just the two of them now—dangling off the edge of the table.

"You—ba—ca—wa—you—ca—wa—ba—you!" he spluttered.

"Yes, I know what you mean," she said, beaming. Her brown eyes were lively behind their rather smeary glasses. Now Josh sat up, making similar noises.

"I know exactly what you want to say. Why on earth would I change you both into spiders, yes? Well—I didn't—not deliberately. I was having a crack at changing your little pee-soaked dog into a spider, I admit. But then you two blundered in and got the S.W.I.T.C.H. spray on your legs instead. You know, I *did* try to stop you from running off into danger. You're lucky to be alive. If I hadn't found you in time, stamped on that toad, frightened those rats off, and then whipped you away from that blackbird, you'd be floating in some creature's digestive juices by now."

"Well, thanks!" muttered Josh.

"How *did* you find us?" asked Danny. "We were tiny!"

"Aah!" Petty Potts held up a small device that looked a bit like a mini flashlight. A blue light flashed on the end of it. It gave off a crackly noise. "This is a S.W.I.T.C.H.ee detector. It only works within about ten feet of a S.W.I.T.C.H.ed creature, but it's a help when they wander off. It gets brighter and louder, the closer I get."

"You do realize we could be dead by now—

thanks to you?" said Danny, glaring at her. "Or if your gadget thingy hadn't worked, we'd be spiders for life!"

"No, you wouldn't. The S.W.I.T.C.H. spray doesn't last." Petty Potts sighed and shook her head. "I haven't quite perfected it. But I also have an antidote for emergencies, which I just used on you. Thought you might like a little snack first, though. So I dropped in a couple of flies, already prepared by another spider behind my fridge. I guess it was Danny who scoffed one, wasn't it?" Danny nodded, looking a little green. "So—tell me! What does it taste like?" She perched on a stool and stared at him. Danny stared back at her, horrified.

"And how was it? To be a spider? It must have been so exciting!" She was nodding and smiling at both of them now. There was a notebook and a pen in her hand. "SPIDER-SWITCH is my latest spray. I wasn't sure it would work, as it's an arachnid serum, not an insect one. And of course, I've never tried any of my S.W.I.T.C.H. sprays on mammals until today. So—what does it feel like?"

Danny snapped. He jumped off the table. "What do you think it feels like, you crazy witch?" he squawked. "Terrifying, that's what! We've been nearly flattened, drowned, eaten, and pecked to death!"

Petty Potts sighed again and nodded some more. "I can see it's been a bit upsetting for you. Why don't you come to tea tomorrow and tell me all about it then?"

"You must be joking!" said Danny. "We will NEVER, EVER set foot on this side of the fence again. EVER. And don't you ever come over our to side! If you want to find out what it feels like to be changed into a spider, S.W.I.T.C.H. yourself!"

They jumped off the table. They ran back home barefoot, scraping through the gap in the fence at high speed and never looking back.

Back in her lab, Petty Potts smiled to herself. She picked up a little red velvet box from a high shelf. She lifted the lid, revealing six shiny glass cubes. Each had a tiny hologram of an insect or bug inside it and a series of strange symbols running along beneath it. Danny would have recognized

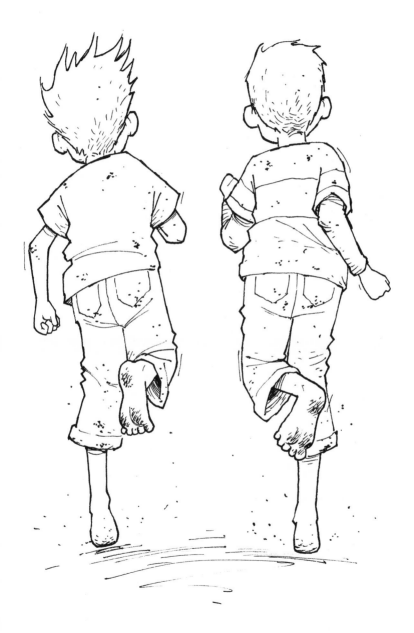

them. Last week he had been to an ancient Egypt exhibition with school. He would have said they were "hieroglyphics"—the mini pictures that made up the ancient Egyptian alphabet. To Petty, though, these were "code." The most amazing code to the most astonishing formula in the world, if you know how to crack it. And Petty knew.

Petty ran her fingers lovingly across the cubes before closing the box. She returned it to the shelf. Then she picked up the green velvet box beside it. She opened this one with a sigh. Inside was a single glass cube with a tiny lizard hologram inside it and more of the hieroglyphics. There were five other square dents. Empty.

Petty's smile vanished. She thwacked her forehead with her palm. "Oh, you stupid, stupid old woman! Had to get your memory burnt out, didn't you?! What if you NEVER find them again, eh? Then you'll never get the *next* code. And you'll never get any further than bugs!"

Hair Today

"Danny! I can't believe you're not eating your cake!" said Mom. She stared at Danny's uneaten dessert in astonishment.

Danny gave her a wobbly smile. "Um—it's just that I'm still full since . . . since . . . lunch." When he remembered what he'd last eaten, his smile went even more wobbly.

"He ate the insides of a bluebottle earlier," said Josh, through a mouthful of his chocolate cake. Danny flinched. "It wasn't quite dead, either."

"Ooh—you two are so revolting and creepy," shuddered Jenny. Her hair was still wrapped up in a towel. She'd only got out of the bath five minutes ago. She could set a world record for staying in a bath, reading magazines. "Stop talking about disgusting things, or I'll kill you both!"

"Not again," moaned Danny. "You've already tried twice today."

He got up and went into the yard with his cake. He went to the shed, knelt down, and then put the plate down next to it. Josh followed him. "What are you doing?" he asked.

"Seeing if Scratch and Sniff are in," said Danny. "They told us they live under our shed, remember?"

"Oh yeah," said Josh. He sat down next to Danny. "We never did thank them for saving our lives."

Behind him there were squeaks and then the familiar snouts of Scratch and Sniff emerged. They twitched at the lovely scent in the air.

"This is to say thanks," said Danny. He tipped the cake off the plate. "You probably can't really work out what I'm saying. But thanks anyway. For looking after me and Josh." Sniff clasped her little paws together. She rolled her eyes with delight. "No frosting on it," said Danny.

"See you around," said Josh. Their friends bit into the cake and dragged the whole thing back under the shed with little grunts of effort and delight.

"Maybe we won't," said Danny. "I think we should probably just forget the whole thing! Nothing like that will ever happen again. We've boarded up the fence so Piddle can't get through. And we will never go next door—ever again."

"So right," said Josh. "I love wildlife. But I don't want to *be* it."

Danny and Josh ran inside. Jenny was holding her hair dryer. The cord was stretched around to the outlet just outside the downstairs bathroom where she liked to do her hair and makeup. She stalked out and ripped the plug out of the socket, huffing and glaring at Mom through a curtain of wet hair.

"How many times do I have to tell you, Jenny?" snapped Mom. "STOP drying your hair over the sink."

"NO!" shouted Danny. "Let her! Let her dry her hair over the sink! It saves lives!"

Jenny and Mom stared at him—and at Josh who was nodding vigorously in agreement.

"I tell you, Mom," said Jenny. She pointed at them with the hair dryer. "They're another species, these two. Another species!"

Top Secret!

For Petty Potts's Eyes Only!!

DIARY ENTRY *562.4

SUBJECT: Josh and Danny Phillips

Have made a breakthrough! Those ghastly eight-year-olds from next door got sprayed by mistake! Managed to rescue them, though, before they got eaten. Asked what being a spider was like, but they were hysterical. Will try again tomorrow.

Good news! They can't get away from me. They live next door. And as they are children, nobody will ever believe what happened, so my secret is safe. And anyway, I think it's high time I had some assistants on the S.W.I.T.C.H. PROJECT. I've been working alone for far too long.

REMEMBER

$$\frac{4 \times \pi^2}{0S-7} * \quad \frac{P_2}{0.8} \times \frac{\sqrt{6^2 0/9}}{9.\sqrt{5^\circ_T}} = \frac{4.198}{4.197} \atop (548)$$

If ONLY I could REMEMBER what happened to the rest of my research! I know I put the code for S.W.I.T.C.H.ing creatures to reptiles in the crystal cubes, as I did for the bugs and insects formula . . . and I know I hid the cubes somewhere safe. Too safe. Safe from even me!!! I just can't remember. Victor Crouch has a lot to answer for. I will get my revenge on him for burning out chunks of my memory and trying to steal my life's work. If I ever see him again, I will S.W.I.T.C.H. him into a cockroach and stamp on him.

But with two young brains to help me, I might be able to find the lost reptile S.W.I.T.C.H. cubes and finally rediscover all my brilliant work.

I will recruit Josh and Danny tomorrow. I am sure I can persuade them to help me with my research, and also to continue the hunt for the missing cubes.

Yes, I am sure I will find a way to convince them.

After all . . . what boy wouldn't want to transform into a giant python or a crocodile one day . . . ?

$$\frac{60}{\text{OUP}} \cdot \pi \rightarrow \text{\$} \rightarrow \frac{1}{2} s t \qquad \rightarrow \qquad \text{ARACHNID}$$

Glossary

abdomen: the main part of a spider's body

antidote: a medicine that can reverse the effects of a poison

arachnid: another name for a spider. Arachnids are joint-legged (they have more than one joint on each leg) and are invertebrates (animals without spines)

cellular: something made from a group of living cells

hieroglyphics: ancient Egyptian pictures and symbols that represent words

hijack: to take control of something by force

hologram: a picture made up of laser beams that appear three-dimensional (3-D)

insects: animals with six legs and three body parts: the head, thorax, and abdomen

mammals: animals that give birth to live young and feed them with their own milk. Humans and rats are mammals.

mandibles: a spider's mouthparts that are used for clutching food

morphing: the process by which an object changes into something else. For example, Danny and Josh morph from boys into spiders.

nocturnal: animals that hunt at night and rest during the day

omnivore: an animal that can eat plants or other animals. Humans are omnivores.

palps: feelers that spiders use to search for food

prey: an animal that is hunted by another animal for food

reptiles: cold-blooded animals. Lizards and snakes are reptiles.

scavengers: animals that gather things discarded by others or that eat the remains of prey left by another animal

thorax: the section of a spider's body between the head and abdomen

venom: poison that can be squirted from the fangs of an animal to kill or stun its prey. Some spiders are venomous.

Recommended Reading

BOOKS

Want to brush up on your bug knowledge? Here's a list of books dedicated to creepy-crawlies.

Glaser, Linda. *Not a Buzz to Be Found*. Minneapolis: Millbrook Press, 2012.

Heos, Bridget. *What to Expect When You're Expecting Larvae: A Guide for Insect Parents (and Curious Kids)*. Minneapolis: Millbrook Press, 2011.

Markle, Sandra. Insect World series. Minneapolis: Lerner Publications, 2008.

WEBSITES

Find out more about nature and wildlife using the websites below.

BioKids

http://www.biokids.umich.edu/critters/
The University of Michigan's Critter Catalog has

a ton of pictures of different kinds of bugs and information on where they live, how they behave, and their predators.

National Geographic Kids
http://video.nationalgeographic.com/video/kids/animals-pets-kids/bugs-kids
Go to this fun website to watch clips from National Geographic about all sorts of creepy-crawlies.

U.S. Fish & Wildlife Service
http://www.fws.gov/letsgooutside/kids.html
This website has lots of activities for when you're outside playing and looking for wildlife.

CHECK OUT ALL OF THE

#1 Spider Stampede

Eight-year-olds Josh and Danny discover that their neighbor Miss Potts has a secret formula that can change people into bugs. Soon enough, they find themselves with six extra legs. Can the boys survive in the world as spiders long enough to make it home in time for dinner?

#2 Fly Frenzy

Danny and Josh are avoiding their neighbor because she "accidentally" turned them into bugs. But when their mom's garden is ruined the day before a big competition, the twins turn into bluebottle houseflies to discover the culprits. Will they find who's responsible before it's too late?

#3 Grasshopper Glitch

Danny and Josh are having a normal day at school . . . until! they turn into grasshoppers in the middle of class! Can they avoid being eaten during their whirlwind search to find the antidote? And will they be able to change back before getting a week of detention?

 **TITLES!**

#4 Ant Attack

Danny and Josh are being forced to play with Tarquin, the most annoying boy in the neighborhood. But things get dangerous when the twins accidentally turn into ants and discover that Tarquin kills bugs for fun. . . . Can they find a safe place to hide until they turn human again?

#5 Crane Fly Crash

When Petty Potts leaves town, she puts Danny and Josh in charge of some of her S.W.I.T.C.H. spray. Unfortunately, their sister, Jenny, mistakes it for hair spray and ends up as a crane fly. Now it's up to the twins to keep Jenny from being eaten alive.

#6 Beetle Blast

Danny is forced to go with his brother, Josh, to his nature group, but neither of them thought they would turn into the nature they were studying! Both brothers become beetles just in time to learn about pond dipping . . . from the bug's perspective. Can they avoid getting caught by the other kids?

About the Author

Ali Sparkes grew up in the woods of Hampshire, England. Actually, strictly speaking, she grew up in a house in Hampshire. The woods were great but lacked basic facilities like sofas and a well-stocked fridge. Nevertheless, the woods were where she and her friends spent much of their time, and so Ali grew up with a deep and abiding love of wildlife. If you ever see Ali with a large garden spider on her shoulder, she will most likely be screeching, "AAAARRRGHGETITOFFME!"

Ali lives in Southampton with her husband and sons. She would never kill a creepy-crawly of any kind. They are more scared of her than she is of them. (Creepy-crawlies, not her husband and sons.)

About the Illustrator

Ross Collins's more than eighty picture books and books for young readers have appeared in print around the world. He lives in Scotland and, in his spare time, enjoys leaning backward precariously in his chair.